DK READERS

STAR WARS™
A Queen's Diary

BEGINNING
2
TO READ ALONE

Written by Simon Beecroft

My name is Padmé Amidala.

I am the Queen of my planet.

Today I am going to start a diary.

I am going to start a diary because
my life is very busy.

I do not want to forget anything.

My world

If people read this diary
in the future, they might
not know about my world.
So I am going to explain
interesting things about
my world in these boxes.

A Note to Parents and Teachers

DK READERS is a compelling programme for beginning readers, designed in conjunction with literacy experts, including Maureen Fernandes, B.Ed (Hons). Maureen has spent many years teaching literacy, both in the classroom and as a literacy specialist in schools.

Beautiful illustrations and superb full-colour photographs combine with engaging, easy-to-read stories and informational texts to offer a fresh approach to each subject in the series.

Each DK READER is guaranteed to capture a child's interest while developing his or her reading skills, general knowledge and love of reading.

The five levels of DK READERS are aimed at different reading abilities, enabling you to choose the books that are exactly right for your child:

Pre-level 1: Learning to read

Level 1: Beginning to read

Level 2: Beginning to read alone

Level 3: Reading alone

Level 4: Proficient readers

The "normal" age at which a child begins to read can be anywhere from three to eight years old. Adult participation through the lower levels is very helpful for providing encouragement, discussing storylines and sounding out unfamiliar words.

No matter which level you select, you can be sure that you are helping your child learn to read, then read

LONDON, NEW YORK,
MELBOURNE, MUNICH, AND DELHI

Project Editor Laura Gilbert
Designer Jon Hall
Brand Manager Lisa Lanzarini
Publishing Manager Simon Beecroft
Category Publisher Siobhan Williamson
Production Nick Seston
DTP Designer Santosh Kumar G

Lucasfilm
Executive Editor Jonathan W. Rinzler
Art Director Troy Alders
Continuity Supervisor Leland Chee

Literacy Specialist
Maureen Fernandes

First published in Great Britain in 2007 by
Dorling Kindersley Limited,
80 Strand, London WC2R 0RL

2 4 6 8 10 9 7 5 3 1
SD335 – 8/07

A CIP catalogue record for this book
is available from the British Library.

ISBN: 978-1-40532-780-0

Colour reproduction by Wyndeham Pre-Press Ltd., UK
Printed and bound in China by L Rex Printing Co., Ltd.

Discover more at
www.dk.com

www.starwars.com

Today I tried to count all the rooms in the palace, where I live.
I quickly lost count.
My palace is so large I think I shall never be able to explore all of it.

I love to climb up to one of the highest rooms.
Then I gaze at the waterfalls that flow down the side of the mountain.

Home world

I live on a planet called Naboo.
Naboo is a small planet.
It is very beautiful.

Today a lot of important people visited me.

When people meet me, some of them are surprised that I am so young.

I am just 14 years old.

All queens on my planet are young.

I am not even the youngest!

Even though I am not very old, I want to be a good queen.

Landspeeder

This morning I flew in a landspeeder.
I love travelling fast in landspeeders.
I flew around the city and looked at
all the pretty buildings.
Lots of people waved at me.

My palace is in the biggest city on Naboo, but I have not always lived here.

I was born in a mountain village.

People of Naboo

The humans who live on my planet are called the Naboo. I am one of them. The Naboo live in cities and villages.

I was learning about the Gungans
in my lessons today.
I learnt that the Gungans also
live on my planet.
They live in underwater cities.
The Gungans can also live on land.
I would like to meet a Gungan.

Naboo natives

The Naboo and the Gungans do not often meet each other. They are not enemies, but they are not friends either!

Gungan   *Naboo*

I often think about my
parents and sisters.
I have many memories
of growing up
in my village.

When I was young,
my teachers realised
I was very clever.
My teachers gave me
extra training.
Later, people
decided to vote for
me as Queen.
It was the proudest
day of my life!

Padmé

14

Sola

Ruwee

Jobal

Eirtaé

Rabé

I have handmaidens who look
after me and help me dress.
They also protect me from danger.

My handmaidens are my friends, too.
Eirtaé (pronounced AIR-TAY) and
Rabé are two of my
closest handmaidens.

Royal dress

On my planet,
kings and queens
wear special clothes
and make-up.
They also wear their
hair in special ways.

Today I am going to visit a nearby planet in my special spaceship. My spaceship is totally silver.

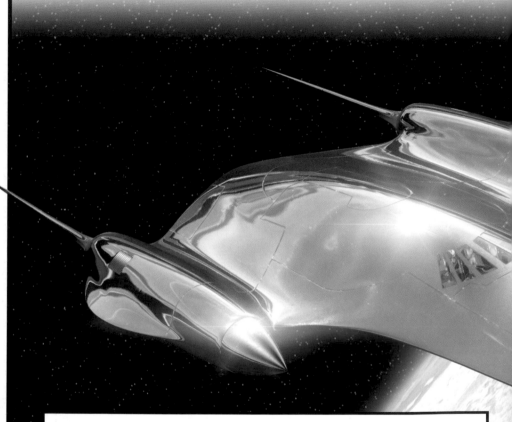

Spaceships

Naboo kings and queens fly silver spaceships. There is even a throne in my ship!

It has large rooms inside.
No one has a spaceship like mine.
I am even learning to fly it.

Sabé

Sometimes it is hard being Queen,
because everyone knows me.
Sabé is my best friend and
one of my handmaidens.

Padmé

Sometimes Sabé dresses as me, and
I dress as a handmaiden.
We have a secret way of talking
in code when we are in disguise.

A terrible thing has happened.
My planet has been invaded.
Enemy soldiers tried to capture me,
but I was saved by two Jedi Knights.
I had never met a Jedi before, but
I had heard about them.
They travel everywhere to help
people in need.

Droid soldiers

The enemy soldiers are machines called droids. Every droid soldier is armed and dangerous.

Now we are flying away from my planet to search for help for my people.

We have landed on a planet
to repair the spaceship.
The planet is rough and dry.
We went to a local town.
I went in disguise so no one
would know I was a queen.
I met a boy who is a slave.
This means that someone
owns him, and he is not free
to ever leave his master.

This young boy is very special.

His name is Anakin and he told me

I looked like an angel.

I think we will be friends.

The Jedi think that
Anakin is special.
They think that he
might have special
powers, like a Jedi.
They want to free
him from slavery, so
he can learn how to
be a Jedi.

Amazing news! Anakin is free!
He won a dangerous race in his
Podracer to gain his freedom.
Now we can get help for my planet.

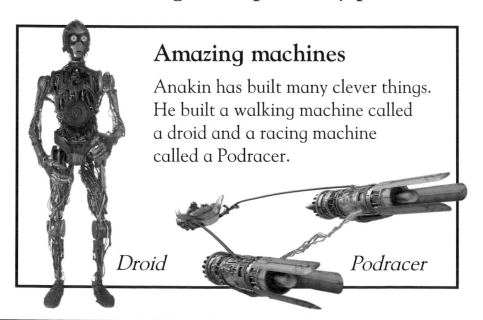

Amazing machines

Anakin has built many clever things.
He built a walking machine called
a droid and a racing machine
called a Podracer.

Droid

Podracer

Today I became a fighter.
No one would help my people, so
I had to help them myself.
I went with the Jedi to ask the
Gungans for help.

Together we made an army and fought the enemy droid soldiers. The Gungans fought bravely, but many of them died.

Weapons
The Gungans use many weapons in battle, including giant catapults.

My planet is free!

Anakin helped us a lot.

He flew a spaceship straight into the

invaders' spaceship and blew it up!

Although it was really an accident,

when Anakin destroyed the ship the

droids could no longer fight.

Now I'm sure Anakin

will be trained as a Jedi.

Perhaps we will

meet again....

Places I have visited

I travelled to the
swamps on my planet.
The Gungans
have a secret
meeting place there.

I visited a dangerous planet
called Tatooine with
the Jedi Qui-Gon Jinn.
We went to a busy town.

When I was visiting Tatooine,
I watched a fast sporting race
called a Podrace.
A huge crowd gathered
to watch the race.

I flew to the centre of the galaxy to visit the capital planet.
One enormous city covers the entire planet.